Run Like The Wind belongs to:

Text copyright © 2005 Heather Henning
Illustrations copyright © 2005 Gillian Chapman

Published in Ireland by O'Donnell Press 2005,
12 Coolemoyne Park, Jordanstown, Co. Antrim BT37 0RP
Telephone: 028 9096 6493
Email address: b.odonnell93@ntlworld.com

A CIP catalogue record of this book is available from the British Library.

Printed in Ireland by GPS Colour Graphics Ltd.
Repro Scanning by iris colour.

ISBN 0-9546163-6-7

Run Like The Wind

By Heather Henning
Illustrated by Gillian Chapman

O'DONNELL PRESS

Ollie the young ostrich
loved to walk by the cool water.
He loved to sit in the shade,

but most of all
he loved to race with his brothers and sisters.
"Look, Mum!" he said. "I can run the fastest!"

One day Ollie ran so fast that he left his little family
far behind. In the hills he was...ALONE.
Then he heard a strange sound. Roaring and
streaks of lightning threatened to tear the sky in two.
"I'm frightened!" cried Ollie. "The sky is shaking!"
With drooping feathers, he crouched under the nearest bush...

...and hid there until the storm had passed.
"Clumsy clump of feathers, now look what you've done!"
cried a red-headed weaver bird, dropping a twig
from its beak. Ollie looked up.
"Who are you?"

"I'm a busy weaver bird
and I see everything that goes on around here.
WHO ARE YOU?"

"I'm Ollie, the fastest running bird!"

"Bird?" chuckled the red-headed weaver.

"Can you hop, light as a feather, from branch to branch?
Can you flutter your wings? Can you FLY?"

Ollie fluttered, but he COULD NOT FLY.

"I CAN'T FLY!" cried Ollie. "Then who *am* I?"

"You must go and find out," chirped the weaver bird.

Ollie walked and walked, until he met a friendly giraffe.
"Where are you going, little one?" asked the giraffe.
"To find out who I am," said Ollie.
"Please may I come along with you?"
"You have a lovely long neck like me," said Giraffe,
"but where are the patterns on your coat,
and WHERE IS YOUR TAIL?"
"Tail?" said Ollie, jumping back. "I have no TAIL!"
and on he ran ...

...until he came to the river,
where the playful elephant
was SPLASHING.
"Where are you going?" said
the elephant.
"To find out who I am," said Ollie.

"Please may I splash in the river with you?"
"You have long legs for splashing," said the elephant,
"but where are your tusks... and your TRUNK?"
"Trunk?" said Ollie. "I have no TRUNK!"
and on he ran...

...over the grassy plain, until he met a smart young zebra.
"Where are you going?" said the zebra.
"To find out who I am," said Ollie.
"Please may I come along with you?"
You have strong feet for running," said the zebra,
"but where are your pretty stripes?"
"Stripes?" said Ollie. "I have no STRIPES!"
and away he ran!

"Grrr!" said a huge lion stretching out in the grass,

"Where are you off to, little one?"
"To find out who I am," said the young ostrich.
"Please may I stay here with you?"
"You have a big mouth for calling," said the lion,
"but can you toss your mane like this and roar
like GRRRR...!"
The ground shook and Ollie ran as
fast as an ostrich could.

He ran and ran until...
"Where are you going, little one?" said a sly cheetah.
"To find out who I am," said Ollie.
"Ooh," said the cheetah, "you can come along with me,
and we could RACE together."

"I'd love to race," said the young chick.
Ollie and the cheetah ran side by side.

"OUCH!" cried Ollie. "You stood on my feathers!"
Ollie turned his head and there right behind him
was the largest mouth of spiky teeth!
"SNARL," said the cheetah.
"HELP!" squealed Ollie, running faster than ever...

...into the sound of THUMPITY-THUD!
And from a dense cloud of dust
came a flock of large ostriches racing towards Ollie.

"Leave the chick alone!" stormed Mother Ostrich.
"Leave him alone!" thundered the flock.
Startled, Cheetah turned and fled
and disappeared as any sly cheetah would.

"My little chick, we've been looking for you," said Mother Ostrich.
"Where have you been?"

"Away...to find out who I am," said Ollie.
"You're an OSTRICH BIRD!" said his mother.
"Bird?" said Ollie. "But I can't fly like a bird."
"You don't need to fly.
We ostriches run like the wind!"
"But...can we chase the lightning out of the sky?" laughed Ollie,
running along at his mother's side.